Starlight

Gillian Lobel
Illustrated by Nic Wickens

Tamarind Ltd

Sponsored by **NASUWT**

**For
Joseph, Theo, Ana
and Jack**

**With thanks to
Sutay**

"Happy Birthday to you!" said Grandma and held out Araba Rose's present. It was a very strange parcel.

Grandma called her Rosie, and was always making her astonishing presents.

Once she knitted her a hot-air balloon, with three little people in the basket, all ready to take off.

"What is it, Grandma?" asked Rosie, with a giggle.

"Go on. Unwrap it and see," smiled Mum.

"It's a hobby-horse!" cried Rosie.

"Thanks Grandma. He's lovely!"

The hobby-horse's head was as green as the sea.
He had starry eyes and his mane sparkled like the sun on water.

"What will you call him?" asked Grandma.

"Starlight," said Rosie, and held him tight.

Rosie took Starlight to bed with her that night.
Mum tucked her up and drew the curtains.

"Not too close!" said Rosie

The moon shone into the room and bathed the hobby-horse's head
in a pool of light.

"Good-night Starlight," whispered Rosie,
as she drifted off to sleep.

Was it the moonlight, or did the hobby-horse blink a starry eye?

"Rosie, Rosie."

"Who's that?" asked Rosie and she sat up.
It was Starlight, whispering in her ear.

"You can talk!"

"Of course I can!" said Starlight.
"Would you like to go on a flying adventure?"

"A flying adventure?" whispered Rosie. "Girls can't fly."

"They can if they come with me," said Starlight.
"Climb on and hold my reins tightly."

Her bedroom slid away as they soared through the air.
Up among the stars they flew, while the moon shone down
on the gardens below and a river
coiled in the valley like a snake.

"Where are we going?" shouted Rosie.

"To the North," Starlight replied.

Rosie looked down and saw the sea beneath her,
the tiny waves flashing like dragonfly
wings in the moonlight.

Down, down they flew
over icebergs
like shining
castles
in the
sea.

Suddenly the air blossomed
with snowflakes like cold, soft daisies.
Rosie laughed and reached out to catch one.

She shivered as they went spinning away
on the wind.

"Time to go home!" said Starlight.

They took one last look, then the hobby-horse
caught a moonbeam and sped back home.

Next morning, Rosie told
her mother all about
her ride with Starlight.

"What a busy night you've
had," said Mum.

"It was magic, Mum,"
Rosie said.

When night came and the moon shone, Starlight shook his mane and turned his silvery eyes to her.

"Rosie, Rosie, shall we fly again?"
"Oh, Starlight. Yes, please. Where shall we go?" she asked.
"To the Kingdom of the Sea," replied Starlight.

Once more her bedroom seemed to melt away, and Rosie was out in the cold night air, clutching Starlight's frosty mane.

Then Rosie saw the sea stretch out below them.
She closed her eyes and shivered.

Starlight swooped steeply, and Rosie held on tight.

"Don't be afraid, Rosie," called Starlight
as the wind whistled through his mane.
"I will keep you safe."

Rosie felt the waves slide over her.
It was blissfully warm.
When she opened her eyes she was in a pale,
green watery world.
Fish swam all around her.

"Let's follow them," whispered Starlight,
and off they sped through streams of silver bubbles.

Rosie caught sight of a strange little creature
beside them.

"It's a little horse like you, Starlight," she cried.

"It's my cousin, the sea-horse," replied Starlight.

"Welcome!" called
the sea-horse.

"Sorry I can't stay.
I have my child
to look after."

Suddenly Rosie saw a huge dark shape like a ship
gliding by. Strange whistles and calls
made the water quiver, and a deep voice sounded.

"White Fin, White Fin! I go North, I go North!"

"What's that?" asked Rosie.

"You're safe, Rosie. It's a whale.
They sing all the time, you know."

Soon the water echoed
to the sound
of many deep voices,
singing their strange,
rich songs.

"Can we follow them?"
begged Rosie.

"No, it's time
for us to go home."

Up, up they swam, until they caught a wave.
They rode on its crest, out into the cool night air.

"I'm quite dry!" Rosie shouted, astonished.

"Magic!" murmured Starlight, and he laughed his
silvery laugh.

The next day Rosie's mum was cleaning.

"I can help," said Rosie, "and Starlight can watch."

She put all her things away neatly and dusted all the ornaments on the shelves.

She loved helping. Most of all she loved to use the vacuum cleaner.

She ran round the room
pushing the cleaner.

"I'm the dragon-monster!
The magic dust eater.
Whooooo!"

"Be careful!" her mother called.
"Watch out!"

But it was too late.
The cleaner had snaked its cord around Starlight.

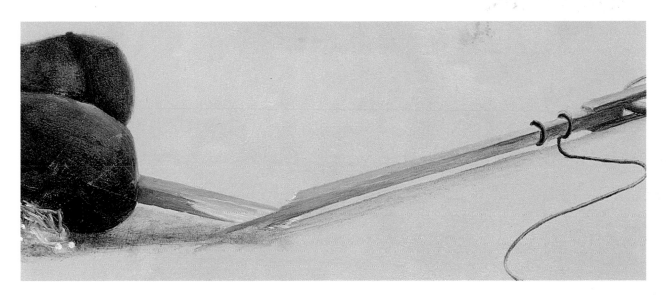

There was a loud crack
and Starlight
lay broken on the floor.
Rosie sobbed as if her heart would break.

"I've hurt him, Mum! I didn't mean to! I didn't!"

"I know," said Mum. "Don't worry Rosie,
I think I can fix him."

Together Rosie and her mother carried
the wounded Starlight downstairs.

Mum found some wood glue from the cupboard.

"He'll be as good as new quite soon, Rosie.
Be gentle with him now," said her mother,
as she wrapped a strong bandage round him.

That night, when Rosie went to bed, she let Starlight rest beside her.

"How are you, Starlight?" she asked.

The hobby-horse gave a faint whinny.
"I'm getting better," he said softly.

"Will you be able to fly again?" asked Rosie.

"Oh Rosie, I can never fly again," he said.
"My magic has gone!"

Rosie hugged him and her warm tears trickled onto his bandaged wound.

As Rosie cradled Starlight's head,
a strange thing happened.
She felt Starlight grow soft and warm,
and his breath tickled her cheek.

She looked up.
Starlight the hobby-horse had vanished.
In his place stood
a beautiful silver horse,
whose mane streamed like a river
in the moonlight.

"I'm free!" he cried. "I'm alive.
Your love has made me real, Rosie."

Then Rosie climbed onto Starlight
and out of the window they flew,
wheeling round in the night air,
as bright as the stars above them.

It seemed to Rosie that the stars
sang for joy, and their music
flowed over them.

For hours they flew,
and Rosie hoped it
would never end.

Then Rosie found herself standing under the apple tree in her own garden.

"Dear Rosie, I must go now," said Starlight.

"Why, oh why?" cried Rosie. "Don't leave me!"

"I must go back to my own land, now that I am free," replied Starlight gently. "But sometimes when the stars are bright, I will return."

A light breeze wafted around her
and Rosie was back in her bedroom.

She rushed to the window and looked out.

"Look for me by starlight,"
called a voice from the dark, spangled sky.

On the nights when the stars are bright,
Starlight returns to take Rosie on an adventure.

Sometimes to the North
sometimes to the South
sometimes on land
sometimes at sea

and always
on her birthday.

OTHER TAMARIND TITLES

Dizzy's Walk
Mum's Late
Rainbow House
Marty Monster
Zia the Orchestra
Jessica
Where's Gran?
Toyin Fay
Yohance and the Dinosaurs
Time for Bed
Dave and the Tooth Fairy
Kay's Birthday Numbers
Mum Can Fix It
Ben Makes a Cake
Kim's Magic Tree
Time to Get Up
Finished Being Four
ABC – I Can Be
I Don't Eat Toothpaste Anymore
Giant Hiccups
Boots for a Bridesmaid
Are We There Yet?
Kofi and the Butterflies
Abena and the Rock – Ghanaian Story
The Snowball Rent – Scottish Story
Five Things to Find –Tunisian Story
Just a Pile of Rice – Chinese Story

For older readers, ages 9 – 12
Black Profiles Series
Benjamin Zephaniah
Lord Taylor of Warwick
Dr Samantha Tross
Malorie Blackman
Baroness Patricia Scotland
Mr Jim Braithwaite

A Tamarind Book

Published by Tamarind Ltd, 1999

Text © Gillian Lobel
Illustrations © Nic Wickens
Edited by Simona Sideri

ISBN 1 870516 43 5

Designed and typeset by Judith Gordon
Printed in Singapore